W9-ALN-739

A HORSE CALLED
COURAGE

Anne Schraff

PAGETURNERS

Development and Production: Laurel Associates, Inc.

SADDLEBACK
EDUCATIONAL PUBLISHING
www.sdlback.com

ISBN-13: 978-1-56254-187-3
ISBN-10: 1-56254-187-0
eBook: 978-1-60291-226-7

Printed in the United States of America
15 14 13 12 11 10   2 3 4 5 6 7 8 9

CONTENTS

Chapter 1

"Just think of it! We can spend the summer working with horses and get *paid* for it, too!" Sommer Oldham cried excitedly.

Vanessa Downey grabbed Sommer's hand and said, "You *sure* they'll hire us? Are you totally sure?"

"Yes," Sommer smiled. "My uncle owns the summer camp. He said he needs several teenage counselors to work with the little kids."

Standing nearby, Tami Nguyen smiled, too. Sommer and Vanessa were not *her* best friends, but they were best friends with each other. Tami hadn't had a best friend in high school. She was so shy she didn't have any close friends. Sometimes Tami tagged along after Vanessa and Sommer, but they always talked to each other and pretty much ignored her.

"How about you, Tami? You're coming to work at Camp Colorado, too, aren't you?" Vanessa asked. "I promised my uncle I could get two other girls beside myself."

"Oh, yes," Tami said in surprise at being asked. She needed the money very badly. But she didn't share the excitement and happiness of the other two girls. Tami feared being so far from home for the first time. Worse yet, she was terrified of horses!

The part of town where Tami lived was nicknamed "Little Vietnam." Along with her parents, grandfather, and her three brothers and sisters, she felt very safe and comfortable there. But next September Tami would be starting college, and she needed to earn some money this summer. The Nguyen family had been struggling ever since they came to the United States when Tami's parents were teenagers. Tami was determined to pay for her own education.

"Grandfather," Tami said that night, "I think I can get a summer job at a children's camp. A girl I know from school is arranging it."

"Excellent," Grandfather said. Decades ago, just after the war, he had escaped from Vietnam in a flimsy boat. Many of those with him had drowned, and many were killed by pirates. But Grandfather and Grandmother had made it to the United States. With them they brought the teenaged neighbor boy who would become Tami's father.

"But I'm a little scared, Grandfather. Camp Colorado is a long way up in the mountains—perhaps 100 miles from home," Tami said.

"We came to this new land over *thousands* of miles," Grandfather said with a smile. "You have not that far to go, dear child."

"I know, I know," Tami said, "but I am afraid of horses, too, and we'll have to ride the horses there."

"You must not let fear control you, Tami," Grandfather scolded. "You must say to yourself over and over that you will be brave."

A few days later, everyone applying for jobs at the camp gathered for interviews. Tami filled out the application, and tried to hide her fear when she spoke to the camp director. Like Sommer and Vanessa, Tami was hired immediately.

One week later all the camp employees boarded a bus headed for Camp Colorado. Tami didn't know any of the passengers on the bus except Vanessa and Sommer. And of course those two girls shared a seat, talking constantly to one another. So Tami sat alone, looking out the window. She didn't blame the girls for not paying attention to her. They had much more in common with each other than they did with her. Tami concentrated on feeling grateful that this job would help her earn money for college.

The sun was shining brightly as the bus full of chattering teenagers rolled through traffic. All along the way, however, Tami fought the desire to crawl away and hide. She had never been comfortable with strangers.

"Isn't this exciting, Tami?" Vanessa said as the bus began climbing the steep mountain road. It was the first time today that she had talked to Tami.

"Oh, yes," Tami said, trying to sound enthusiastic. But in truth she was more frightened than excited. If she had been going camping with her family, she would have been *truly* happy.

Tami felt miserable. She knew that tonight her parents and brother and sisters would sit down to a fine meal of chao, chicken, and long rice soup. For dessert there would be delicious moon cakes made from sweet rice filled with bananas and raisins. They would all be warm and friendly with each other and have a pleasant, comfortable evening.

With her whole heart, Tami wished she could be there with them. As the bus climbed the winding mountain road, Tami felt sadder about each mile that took her farther from home.

Chapter 2

It was midmorning when the bus reached the campgrounds. Camp Colorado was a beautiful place with many little log cabins and one very large cabin for dining and recreation. A sparkling lake lay amid pine trees at the bottom of a hill. Sad as she was, Tami had to admit to herself that it really was a lovely setting.

When the 20 young people filed from the bus, the camp director met them with a clipboard.

"Hi, guys, I'm Dane Morgan," he said with a smile. He didn't look more than 19 or 20, but he was confident and self-assured. Tami couldn't help but notice that he was very handsome, too. "First thing you need to do is to fill out these papers," he said. "Here's your chance to express your preferences for what kind of work you'd like to do around here. We don't want to put any square pegs in round holes!"

Everybody laughed. All the girls giggled and whispered to each other about how gorgeous Dane Morgan was. He had thick, curly hair and big brown eyes and dimples in his cheeks. Sommer nudged Vanessa and said, "Is he totally cool or what?"

Now Tami looked over the list of available jobs: counselor, horseback riding, sports, crafts, kitchen help, maintenance. Sitting at one of the picnic tables, she quickly checked "kitchen help." Yes, she would probably be happiest cutting up vegetables and running the dishwasher.

Vanessa and Sommer looked over at Tami. "We're putting horseback riding as first choice," Vanessa said. "That's the most fun. Be sure to write that down, too, Tami." Tami had never admitted her fear of horses to the other girls. One day, when all three of them had gone riding in the park, Tami had been terrified the whole time. It didn't matter that her horse was as gentle as a big pussycat. Tami was ashamed of being such a timid person.

"Everybody will want that," Tami said, "so we may not all get it." Then she quickly folded her paper. It would be embarrassing if everyone saw that she had chosen to work in the kitchen rather than ride a spirited horse over the beautiful trails.

With any luck, Tami thought, she could spend her time here at Camp Colorado slicing vegetables and making salads. That way she could avoid scary horses and strange people altogether.

"I put crafts as my second choice," Sommer said.

"Me, too," Vanessa said. "What did you put for second choice, Tami?"

Tami had written 'maintenance,' thinking she would rather empty trash cans than face the horses or try to teach children how to make papier-mâché chickens. "Crafts, yes," she lied.

"I wonder where Dane spends most of his time?" Sommer wondered out loud. "I'd sign up for *anything* to be where he was!"

"All right, you guys," Dane said, as he returned to collect the papers. "You can spend the next hour finding your quarters and getting settled. Then you'll get your assignments at lunchtime. The little kids don't start arriving until tomorrow—so enjoy the peace and quiet while it lasts. Or, if you'd like, you can go riding or swimming this afternoon."

"Did you hear that?" Sommer whispered. "We can go riding!"

"Yeah," Vanessa said with a grin, looking over at the big corral. Most of the horses were bays, but there were a few black and mixed-color horses and one was silver gray with a white mane.

"Do you see that white beauty?" Sommer cried. "Whoa! It's the color of smoke and its mane is like spun silk. That's the one I'd like to ride!"

"That's Courage," Dane Morgan said. The girls hadn't seen him walk up behind them. "I'm afraid he's a very high-spirited animal. We don't usually like to encourage inexperienced riders to ride him."

"Oh, come on, Dane! We're *excellent* riders!" Sommer said.

Tami thought *all* the horses looked huge and dangerous. But the gray one did seem to be the fiercest of all.

"Do you ride?" Dane asked Tami. For a moment, Tami couldn't believe that the handsome young man was actually talking to her.

"Yes, but not very well," Tami said.

Dane smiled. "Well, that's okay. Being here will give you a good chance to become a better rider."

Vanessa and Sommer were staring at Tami and Dane, wondering why he had stopped to talk to *her*, of all people. There were several Asian teenagers here at Camp Colorado, but Tami was the only Asian girl. Maybe, Sommer thought, that's why Dane noticed her. She was an oddity.

"Are you Vietnamese?" Dane asked, seeming genuinely interested in Tami.

"Yes," Tami said. "I was born here, but my parents came to the United States when they were teenagers."

Dane nodded. "My parents adopted two little girls from Korea five years ago. They had two boys—me and my brother—but they wanted girls, too. Now I've got a six-year-old sister named Tiffany, and one named Brittany, who's seven. They're really cute and a lot of fun."

Tami thought the young man was very nice. It was unusual for her to feel comfortable with a stranger, but she felt at home with him for some reason. Maybe it was because he had such a nice, friendly way about him.

When Dane walked away, Vanessa and Sommer rushed right over to Tami. Sommer had an angry look in her eye. "What's the deal? Do you know that guy from somewhere?" she demanded.

"No. I never saw him before today," Tami said, "but he seems very nice."

"Boy, you really are a big flirt, aren't you, Tami!" Vanessa said in a rude, accusing voice. "You surprise me. I couldn't believe how you were throwing yourself at that guy!"

Chapter 3

Tami was shocked and hurt. "I was *not* flirting," she said defensively. "I was very surprised when he came to talk to me." Tami was amazed that her friends would so quickly turn against her for no good reason. She could tell that they liked the handsome boy themselves. They must be jealous that he was talking to Tami and not to them. But that was not Tami's fault. How could they blame her?

When the assignments were passed out at lunchtime, Tami got kitchen duty and the other girls got riding.

"What'd you get?" Sommer called out to Vanessa across the room. "I got helping the kids with riding class!"

"Me, too," Vanessa said gleefully. "I

bet Dane Morgan is really into horses, too. We'll see a lot of him."

The girls turned to Tami then. "Did you get riding, too?" Sommer asked.

"No, I'll be helping in the kitchen," Tami said.

Sommer and Vanessa exchanged looks. How could Tami have ended up with such a rotten assignment? But they were secretly glad. If Dane was fascinated by her, he sure wouldn't be seeing much of her in the kitchen!

After lunch, Dane was saddling a horse. The teenaged counselors were clustering around him, and Sommer and Vanessa hurried to join them.

Dane smiled at the eager faces and said, "Let's go for a short ride. I'd like to see how well each of you can ride before the kids arrive. Even you guys who aren't signed up to teach riding class should learn how to handle a horse as long as you're here at Camp Colorado."

Tami tried to slip away, but Dane looked at her and said, "I'd like *everybody* in on this."

Tami was trembling at the thought of getting on one of those horses. She was only 5'3" and she weighed 96 pounds. When she mounted a horse, she felt like a doll sitting on top of an elephant. "I . . . I'm kind of afraid of horses," Tami finally admitted.

Sommer snickered behind her hand. She could imagine what a turn-off that would be to Dane. "You're kidding me, Tami," Sommer said loudly enough for Dane to hear. "You're afraid of a nice riding horse at a kids' camp?"

Tami blushed with embarrassment. "Yes, it's the truth," she said. "They are such *big* animals—I just don't feel safe on a horse."

Dane was smiling at a dark-haired girl who rode out of the corral with perfect riding form. "Nice handling!" he shouted. "Nice posture, Kitty!"

Sommer was eager to show Dane her own riding skills. She also thought it would be funny if Dane could see how really awkward Tami was on a horse. Sommer remembered the day they had all gone riding in the park. Tami's back wasn't straight and she was hunched over in an awkward, funny way.

The truth was that Sommer was still smarting from seeing Dane smiling so warmly at Tami. Now she smiled to herself. What would Dane think of the pretty little Asian girl when he saw how stupid she looked in the saddle? Sommer grabbed Tami's hand. "Come on, Tami, let's go," she said. "You can ride okay. It'll be fun."

Vanessa joined in the effort to force Tami up on a horse. Both of them wanted to show her up.

"No . . . please . . . I'm afraid," Tami groaned, trying to pull away.

Tami was confused by her friends'

insistence that she ride. They must be doing this for her own good, she reasoned. They only wanted her to have some fun—they simply couldn't understand anyone who didn't like horseback riding. At that point, it never dawned on Tami that her friends were trying to humiliate her in front of Dane Morgan.

"Tami wants to ride that black horse," Sommer said to Dane. He smiled and brought the horse over.

"Come on, Tami, I'll show you how to mount," Dane said. He helped Tami into the saddle. She was shaking all over, hoping he didn't notice.

"Just hold the reins like this," Dane explained. "Grasp the horse's mane. . ."

Tami felt like she might topple off the saddle at any moment. She heard several of the other girls giggling at her obvious discomfort.

Now humiliation was added to Tami's fear. She could imagine the horse throwing her to the ground and then kicking her in the head. If that happened, she was sure that everybody would laugh even more loudy at her.

Sommer and Vanessa mounted their horses smoothly. They made it a point to ride past where Dane stood.

"Nice hold on the snaffle reins," Dane told Sommer.

"Good, good," he said to Vanessa, "you're using your legs just right to control the horse—good knee pressure on the turns!"

Then, suddenly, Dane's voice rose in alarm. "Tami, no, *no!* You're not balancing right. You're digging *both* knees into the horse and he doesn't know what to do. You're telling him to go left and right at the same time!"

Tami was terrified. The black horse was starting to trot off and she couldn't control him. She didn't know how to stop him. When she yanked on the reins, the horse snorted in rage.

Sommer and Vanessa exchanged amused looks. Tami was making such a fool of herself! Now Dane could see what an inept person she really was.

Dane Morgan ran after Tami's horse, trying to catch up before there was an accident.

"She's making a real mess of it," Sommer snickered to Vanessa.

"Dane is so disgusted! Look at how angry he looks!" Vanessa said.

Finally, Dane caught the reins of the horse and stopped him. He could see tears running down Tami's cheeks as she gasped, "I'm sorry! I'm so sorry!"

Chapter 4

"That's okay," Dane said kindly. "Nobody is *born* a good rider. It takes a lot of practice. This isn't the horse for you anyway, Tami. He's not too patient with inexperienced riders. Blackjack wasn't the best horse to choose. I don't know why you chose him."

He didn't know that Tami *hadn't* chosen the black horse. Sommer had.

Dane helped Tami down from the saddle, taking a firm hold on her arm. "There we go," he said with a warm smile. "When I give you your next riding lesson, you'll be riding Marshmallow. She's a sweetheart. A beginner could do everything wrong and still have a good ride."

Sommer's joy at Tami's wretched

ride quickly turned to anger and frustration. Instead of being disgusted by Tami's lack of skill, Dane Morgan was being extra nice and helpful to her. Her stupidity was *endearing* to him! Kind and reassuring, Dane was patting her on the back, leading her to a bench where he sat her down while he went to get sodas for them.

Dane didn't even go out on the afternoon ride. He stayed behind to comfort Tami.

"Oh, she's clever!" Sommer said bitterly. "Look, she's got Dane wrapped around her little finger, the little witch."

"You think she acted scared on purpose," Vanessa asked, "just to get Dane to pity her?"

"Yeah, I do," Sommer said. "She's really sneaky. She pretended to be frightened just so Dane the gentleman would rescue poor little scared Tami!"

While the rest of the counselors rode off toward the hills, Tami sipped her soda and said to Dane, "I am so ashamed to be afraid of horses. I'm sure they are nice animals. I think almost everybody likes them."

Dane laughed. "It's okay. We're all afraid of *something* or other. Some people are afraid of dogs," he said.

"When I rode with the other girls last year, we went all through the park on the bridle path, but I never liked it," Tami said. "I thought they wouldn't like me if I didn't pretend I loved horseback riding, too. It is not easy for me to make friends, and I didn't want to lose the few I had."

"Well, a lot of people *do* get hurt riding horses. It's like everything else, Tami. You need to know what you're doing. Once you learn to ride well, it's a pretty safe sport," Dane said. "Just relax now, and stay away from the horses for awhile. Then, if you want to take another shot at it, I'll give you some lessons on Marshmallow. Who knows? You might end up enjoying it."

Tami smiled gratefully at the young man. He didn't make fun of her. He didn't make her feel ashamed for being afraid. Tami liked him very much. Back in high school, Tami hadn't dated any boys. Sometimes she went out with a group of boys and girls, but she never had gone on a date with a boy. She had never met a boy she liked well enough to go out with, and her parents thought that was just fine. They said she was too young for dating anyway.

But this Dane Morgan was very different. Tami thought he might be someone she could enjoy spending some time with.

In the evening, the camp staff gathered around tables in the recreation cabin. Dane told all the counselors what they would be doing tomorrow when the children began arriving at camp. Everyone was given tips on how to deal with anxious parents and homesick kids, especially the bullies, the loners, the troublemakers.

Tami was sitting alone at a table when Sommer joined her. Sommer had been burning with curiosity. She *had* to know what happened between Tami and Dane while the other counselors were out riding that afternoon.

"Hi, Tami," Sommer said. "Did you and Dane get everything squared away about horseback riding?"

"Yes. I told him how afraid I was of horses, and he was very kind and understanding," Tami said. "He was very nice to me."

"Yes," Sommer said. "He feels sorry for you because you almost fell off the horse. I just want to warn you, Tami— don't make a nuisance of yourself with Dane, okay? I mean, Vanessa and I brought you along with us. We don't want you to make us look bad. Dane Morgan is a really busy guy. He hasn't got time for somebody who's always whining and carrying on. He has to think about the little kids coming tomorrow instead of holding the hand of some crybaby seventeen-year-old counselor, you know?"

Tami was shocked by the harshness of Sommer's tone. A terrible thought came to her. Had Dane complained to Sommer about her? Had he said that Tami was causing him trouble? He seemed so nice and considerate. Could he have gone behind Tami's back to ridicule her? "Sommer," Tami asked, "did Dane say he was upset with me?"

Sommer shrugged. "Oh, he's too nice to come right out and *say* that, but I overheard him talking to some of the other guys. He was saying that some of the counselors they've hired are more babyish than the little kids." Sommer carefully constructed her lie to sound believable. "He said something about one stupid girl who had messed up with a horse. He said he shuddered to think of such a fool working with the little kids . . ."

Tami felt like somebody had slapped her across the face with a wet towel. Dane had seemed so kind and understanding! But it was all a lie. He was laughing at her and making fun of her to his friends. Now she made up her mind to avoid Dane at all costs.

Tami was assigned to Tepee F, a cabin with room for a counselor and four children. Each cabin was like that. Early on the morning of the second day, Tami met her four charges. The girls ranged in age from 8 to 10. Tami had sisters 10 and 11, so she was sure she could get along with these lively little campers.

Betsy was an athletic 8-year-old, eager to join in the activities. Leah, a lanky, artistic 9-year-old, was most interested in the craft classes. Liz was a chubby, sweet-natured 10-year-old who wanted to swim all day. Aneal, at age 9, seemed to be moody and sure that everybody hated her. Aneal would need the most attention, Tami thought.

"I heard there were rattlesnakes and coyotes in the hills around here," Betsy said. "I sure hope we get to see some of them. Will we, Tami?"

"I'm sure we'll see wildlife on our hikes," Tami said with a smile.

Just then, there was a rap on the cabin door. Tami was surprised to see Dane Morgan standing there. Now it was hard for her to look into those warm brown eyes she had trusted so quickly. Everything was different now that she knew what he had said behind her back.

Chapter 5

"May I talk to you a minute, Tami?" Dane asked.

"Of course," Tami said. Without looking at him, she stepped outside and closed the door behind her. Her heart ached as she remembered the cruel remarks Sommer had reported that afternoon.

"I want to tell you a little about Aneal, one of your girls," Dane said. "She's an unhappy little girl who can't make friends easily. I'm afraid she's been caught in the middle of a really bitter custody fight between her parents. They've both been doing everything in their power to turn her against the other one. She's angry at the world, I'm afraid. So give Aneal a little extra special attention, Tami—because she needs it," Dane said.

"All right, I will," Tami said, still staring at the ground. She could not bear to look directly at Dane.

Dane smiled warmly. "I sense that you have the *simpatico* to reach her if anybody can," he said.

Tami finally looked at him. *Simpatico?* What did that word mean? She had not heard it before. Sommer said Dane had talked about a stupid girl who couldn't handle a horse. Maybe *simpatico* was another word for stupid. "What does *simpatico* mean?" she asked nervously.

"It's a Spanish word that means 'understanding,'" Dane said. "My mom is Hispanic."

"Oh," Tami said, her lips trembling with the mix of emotions she felt. "I want to apologize again for the trouble I had riding that horse. I know it annoyed you very much, and I want you to know how very sorry I am."

"*Annoyed* me?" he asked in surprise, "Not at all. I—"

Tami cut in before he could go on. "A friend told me what you said—that you haven't got time for stupid girls who almost fall off their horses. She told me you said you can't trust them with the children when they do things like that," she said nervously.

Dane looked shocked. "I never said anything like that, Tami! Whoever told you that I did is lying for some reason. I never even *thought* anything like that. Your friend is a liar, Tami. I'm sorry to be so blunt—but that's the way it is!"

Tami hurried back inside the tepee. Now she was totally confused. Would Sommer make up such a thing? *Why?* Tami didn't have to think long before coming up with a reason. Sommer must be *jealous* of Tami! Back in high school, Sommer had wanted the attention of every good-looking boy. She was probably the prettiest girl in the senior class—and she knew it. She thought she was entitled to first choice of all the boys. Now she was angry at Tami for getting attention from Dane!

In the morning, everybody gathered outside for a big pancake, sausage, and egg breakfast. For an hour or so, Tami was busy frying sausages and eggs and flipping flapjacks. When she was finally done, she found a table over on the side and sat down to eat her breakfast. She deliberately chose a place far from Vanessa and Sommer. Two campers from her tepee, Betsy and Leah, sat down at her table.

"You're nice," Betsy said. "I'm glad you're our camp counselor, Tami. You let us stay up a little after dark."

"Yeah," Leah agreed, "and thanks for telling us that great Vietnamese ghost story. That was so cool. You're extra special, Tami."

"She surely is," said a male voice.

Tami hadn't seen Dane come up. Now he was standing right beside her. His paper plate was loaded with pancakes, sausage, and eggs. "May I join you?"

Dane was wearing a big white apron with a pink cartoon pig on the front. Tami thought he looked adorable.

"Sure," Tami said, smiling at him. She had believed him last night when he denied saying those ugly things.

They sat eating for a while, and then Dane wandered off to flip some more flapjacks. The moment he was gone, Betsy and Leah chanted, "Tami has a boyfriend, Tami has a boyfriend!"

Then Betsy giggled, and both little girls said they thought Dane was as handsome as a movie star.

When Betsy and Leah went off to play a game of soccer, Sommer Oldham came walking toward Tami's table. On the way, she stopped at the grill where Dane was working. Tami could hear her lilting voice on the summer breeze.

"Wow, Dane, are you ever looking good this morning! They shouldn't let a guy as cute as you run loose among all these little girls. Pretty soon they'll start squealing and screaming like fans at rock concerts when their idol appears," Sommer said.

Tami could tell that Dane was embarrassed and annoyed. Sommer was too blatant sometimes. One time she had flirted with boys at school so much that she was called into the principal's office for being disruptive. Another time she gave a young male teacher a picture of herself in a skimpy bathing suit. She got in trouble for that, too. Sommer simply couldn't understand why any young guy who saw her didn't fall crazy in love with her.

"The pancakes are really good, aren't they?" Dane said, ignoring Sommer's personal remarks. "And the sausage, too. Are you on the kitchen staff? If so, you've done a great job."

"Me?" Sommer laughed. "I don't get *near* any kitchen, thank you very much. You remember me, don't you? I'm the girl you complimented for riding so well that first day."

"Sorry," Dane said. "Until I get to know you, you girls all look alike to me. But keep up the good work with your riding. The little kids are all eager to get on a horse—and we need good riders to help them."

Sommer did a slow burn. She hated being snubbed. It was unthinkable! Tami remembered the time a beautiful French exchange student had showed up at school. It was in their junior year. All of a sudden the boys in the class, the ones who were usually drooling over Sommer, began to notice Marie. Sommer was furious. She had called poor Marie all the terrible names she could think of behind her back.

Then someone had poured heavy-duty glue into Marie's purse, cementing her lipstick, mirror, and even ID cards together. When Marie had reached in her purse, the sticky glue bonded her two fingers to the mess. She had to go to the school nurse to get the stuff off. The poor girl had been hysterical.

Nobody could ever prove who had committed the ugly prank, but Tami had always believed it was Sommer.

Chapter 6

Tami had some free time when her charges had all vanished to classes in crafts, swimming, and riding. She took a walk around Camp Colorado, even venturing near the corrals. She looked at all the horses, finally spotting Marshmallow—the gentle horse Dane thought she could ride. She was a gentle looking dappled horse with white spots. She was just as big as the others, but her beautiful brown eyes looked peaceful somehow.

Tami climbed the corral fence and gingerly reached out her hand to pat Marshmallow on the nose. It was soft as the smoothest velvet. Marshmallow nickered softly, but then she broke into a trot and Tami jumped back, startled.

"You're such a chicken," snapped a voice behind Tami. "The horse just barely moves, and you almost jump out of your skin!"

"Sommer," Tami said, "why are you being so mean to me? I did nothing to hurt you. You even lied about what Dane said about me. He never said those cruel things!"

Sommer's eyes narrowed. The beauty of her face disappeared as jealousy narrowed her eyes and reddened her skin. With her pretty eyes narrowed to slits, and her cheeks puffed out with rage, she looked downright ugly. "It's just so *disgusting* how you're chasing Dane Morgan. Everybody sees what you're doing! You wear your jeans so tight they look like they're painted on you. We've watched you wriggle around in front of Dane every chance you get," Sommer said.

"My jeans are no different from yours or any of the other girls' jeans,"

Tami said. "I never flirted with Dane. Give me a break, Sommer. I don't know why you are acting like this."

"Well," Sommer said with a toss of her head, "your *boyfriend*, Dane, said to tell you to meet him in the barn. I guess he wants to teach you how to sit on a horse. You'd better hurry over there before he gets impatient."

"If Dane wants to see me, it must be about the girls in my cabin. It must be important," Tami said. She turned and walked toward the barn. Maybe Dane wanted to tell her more about Aneal. The poor little girl did seem very sad. Tami wanted to help her in any way she could.

Reaching the barn, Tami pushed the door open. "Dane?" she called out. It was so dark inside that Tami had to squint, trying to adjust her eyes. She could make out some stacked bales of hay over in the corner, but there was no sign of Dane.

"Dane?" Tami called out again.

Suddenly the narrow barn door filled up with the shape of a horse. Someone had shooed the horse into the barn and slammed the door shut. Now Tami was trapped in the barn with the horse! Then Tami heard the click of a padlock on the outside of the door.

"No!" Tami screamed, backing away from the nervous, snorting horse. She saw that it was the smoke-colored horse. It was the horse called Courage that Dane had said was too spirited for an inexperienced rider.

Courage restlessly pawed the sawdust floor and whinnied excitedly. Tami was terrified of being kicked or trampled by the frightened horse. She tried to climb to safety on the bales of hay, but she couldn't get a footing.

"Help!" Tami screamed. Now Courage was pitching and bucking like a wild bronc in growing fear of the close quarters and the darkness.

Tami didn't see who had shooed Courage into the barn, but she had a good idea who it was. Sommer must have deliberately lied to Tami about Dane calling her to the barn! And now, knowing how scared Tami was of horses, Sommer had apparently trapped her there with the most dangerous horse in the stable!

"Help!" Tami screamed again, as she backed along the walls of the barn, trying to evade the heavy, thrashing hooves. "Help! Somebody *help!"* she cried. She had never been so frightened in all her life. But as loudly as she screamed, her cries for help were lost in the noise of laughing, shouting campers playing in the swimming pool and on the volleyball courts.

Then, suddenly, Courage kicked violently at the barn wall, and a shaft of light came pouring in. Tami rushed over and pushed aside that board and the one next to it. In a moment she was

45

out and scampering across the meadow. She ran toward the first adult she saw and told him that a horse had been locked in the barn and needed to be freed.

Vanessa and Sommer were in the pool, splashing with the children. Tami walked to the edge of the pool and just stood there, staring. Finally Sommer turned and caught her eye. Tami gave her a withering look, and then quickly walked away.

Tami knew what would happen if she told the camp director what Sommer had done. Sommer Oldham would be packing her bags to return to the city before the end of the day. But Tami didn't want to ruin Sommer's job. She needed money for college, too.

Tami decided that from now on she would stay completely away from Sommer and Vanessa. After all, high school was over. They were all going to different colleges in the fall. It made

Tami sad that she would no longer be friends with the two girls she had known all through high school. But there was no other way now. What else could she do?

Chapter 7

As Tami walked toward her tepee, she saw Aneal sitting by herself on a rough bench made from a log.

"Hi, Aneal," Tami said softly. "Why aren't you swimming? The other girls are having lots of fun in the pool."

"I don't like to swim," Aneal said.

"Why don't you join the softball game?" Tami asked.

"I don't want to," Aneal said. "I don't like people. I'd rather sit here by myself and feed the squirrels."

"Don't you like *any* people?" Tami asked with a small smile.

"Nope," Aneal said firmly.

"How come?" Tami asked.

"I'm afraid of them," Aneal said as she twirled one of her dark pigtails and then wrapped it around her finger. "Just when you get to like them, they run off and leave you alone."

"Did somebody important run away from you, Aneal?" Tami asked softly.

"Uh huh," the 9-year-old girl said. "My dad did. Then Mom got a boyfriend and he was pretty nice. He took me riding on his motorcycle. After a while, though, he ran away, too. Then my mom got another boyfriend and they ran off together and left me with my dad. A couple of months later Mom came back, and now she wants me back—but Dad says no. The two of them are fighting all the time, and I don't know where I'm gonna go or anything. So I'm just plain scared to get mixed up with people."

"I'm scared, too," Tami said.

"You are?" Aneal asked in surprise. "Did people run off on you, too?"

"No. I'm a little scared of being with people because I'm shy. I'm always thinking that people won't like me or that I'll make a fool of myself. And I'm scared of horses, too," Tami admitted.

"Scared of horses?" Aneal almost laughed. "Horses are the *best*! How could anybody be afraid of horses? I like horses better than people."

"I bet you're a good rider," Tami said with an encouraging smile.

"Oh, I'm okay, I guess. I *do* love horses, though. I love horses more than anything in the whole world," Aneal said in a serious voice.

"But they're so big—aren't you afraid of being thrown off?" Tami asked. "It's so far down from the saddle to the ground. And what if the horse kicks you?"

Aneal laughed out loud. "You're kidding me! Is *that* what scares you—honest? Oh, that's the funniest thing I ever heard."

Tami was glad she had made Aneal laugh. At least she was having some success as a counselor.

"Maybe someday I won't be afraid of horses," Tami said. "Dane Morgan said there's a real nice horse named Marshmallow. Maybe I'll try to ride her. Maybe then, little by little, I won't be afraid of horses anymore. And maybe someday *you* won't be afraid of people. Not *all* people run away, you know."

"Maybe," Aneal said. After a moment's silence she looked up. "I like to talk to you, Tami. I've been to camp before. I've talked to lots of doctors and stuff, you know, like psy—psy—"

"Psychiatrists?" Tami filled in.

"Yeah, them. But I like talking to you better. Those guys talk funny. They think I'm just a dumb little kid who doesn't know what's good for me and stuff," Aneal said.

Later, as Tami walked past the corrals, she noticed that Courage was in a special enclosure. He had a bandage on his leg. Maybe he had hurt himself when he kicked the board out of the barn wall. Tami caught up to the veterinarian who was checking over all the horses. "Is Courage all right?" she asked him. "He's not badly hurt or anything, is he?"

"He'll be fine. Just got scratched up a little bit, so we're gonna rest him for a while," the man said.

Aneal joined Tami at the corral fence. "Courage is my favorite horse," she said. "Last year when I came here I got to ride him all the way up to Eagle Point. Everybody said he was real spirited—but the two of us got along fine. I want to ride him tomorrow when the first group goes out."

"I don't think Courage will be riding tomorrow," Tami said. "Some mean person locked him in that dark old hay barn today. He got so upset that he kicked a hole in the wall and hurt his leg a little bit."

* * *

Just as Tami had thought, in the morning all the horses were saddled up—except for Courage. Most of the children went on the morning ride, but a few stayed behind to swim or work on crafts projects they had started. Only a skeleton crew of workers stayed behind to keep an eye on the few campers who were left.

Tami didn't go on the ride because she didn't want to take part in any activity that Vanessa and Sommer were involved in. Dane had told Tami that she should go—that she'd do just fine on Marshmallow—but at the last minute Tami had lost her nerve. She just couldn't make herself climb up on one of those big horses.

When Dane Morgan saddled up for the ride, Tami noticed that Sommer was beaming from ear to ear. Here at last was her chance to have a whole day in the outdoors with Dane! Surely that would wake him up to how beautiful and desirable she was! Without that pesky little Tami to distract him, Dane was bound to give in to Sommer's charms. That was her belief and hope, anyway.

As the large group of riders had saddled up and were moving slowly toward the trail, Aneal changed her mind about going. "If Courage can't go, then I won't go either," she said.

"Courage wouldn't mind if you went on another horse and had some fun," Tami said. She thought it would be a shame for the little girl to miss out on the day's adventure when she loved riding so much.

"No," Aneal said. "Anyway, I think my dad is coming to pick me up today. Grandma said that he and his new girlfriend might come get me."

"Would you like that, Aneal?" Tami asked the little girl.

"Yeah. My daddy lives over there in Cottonwood," Aneal said, pointing west, into the foothills. "It's not far. Daddy has horses, too. Maybe he can buy Courage for me. Then we can keep him in Cottonwood so I can ride him when I visit Daddy."

Tami felt sorry for Aneal. She doubted that the little girl's father was coming for her. It was probably just wishful thinking. Maybe he didn't even live in Cottonwood anymore.

"I guess I'll go swimming," Aneal said, walking toward the pool. Three or four children were already splashing around under the watchful eye of a lifeguard.

Tami went to the kitchen. She had to help the cooks cut up vegetables and meat for tonight's big barbecue. When the horseback riders returned in the early evening, they would have shish-kebab for dinner—chunks of meat and vegetables on skewers. The women in the kitchen were not counselors like Tami. They were regular employees.

Today, the only people left at Camp Colorado were the middle-aged cooks and two older men, the lifeguard and an expert in crafts.

After Tami was finished helping in the kitchen, she went to check on Aneal. When she looked for her in the pool, though, she couldn't see her among the bobbing heads. *She wasn't there.*

Tami was alarmed. "Where is Aneal?" she asked the lifeguard.

"She said she was feeling poorly," the man said. "She went back to her tepee to lie down."

Tami hurried to the tepee. "Aneal," she called out as she opened the door. "Are you okay?"

But no one was there to answer her. The tepee was empty.

A note with a neatly printed message was pinned on the pillow of Aneal's bunk.

Dear Tami,

I'm going to Dad's house.
I'm hiking to Cottonwood.
Love ya,
Aneal

Chapter 8

Aneal's note made Tami recoil in shock. She rushed outside and ran to the pool. "Mr. Irwin," she said to the lifeguard, "Aneal is hiking down to Cottonwood by herself! She left a note!"

"Cottonwood?" Mr. Irwin cried. "That's sixty miles west of here—over some rugged canyons and ravines. No way a little kid is gonna make it that far. In fact, it's dangerous for a kid to be out there at all. There's a horse trail leading over there, but . . ."

Tami thought quickly. "Do you ride, Mr. Irwin?" she asked.

"No, I don't. I never rode a horse in my life," Mr. Irwin said.

"Does Mr. Glantz, the craft teacher, ride?" Tami asked hopefully.

"Nope. He's sixty-nine years old—and he's got arthritis. Look, young lady, you're one of the camp counselors, aren't you? I'm sure you could jump on a horse and catch up to the little girl in no time," Mr. Irwin said.

Tami's heart sank. She had never ridden a horse farther than half a mile —and that was on a bridle path in the park! Worse still, the only horse left in the corral was a high-spirited horse with a sore leg! The big white horse would probably refuse to let her ride him, even if she tried!

"I wonder . . . if I followed the trail on foot, could I catch up to Aneal?" Tami asked.

Mr. Irwin shrugged. "Guess you could try. But if that little kid started off a while ago, she could've gone pretty far. She could be in trouble already, tumbling into a ravine or meeting up with a rattlesnake! I'll call the sheriff right now and they'll send a rescue team. But if I were you, young lady, I'd jump on that white horse right quick and take off after that child. The sheriff will come as soon as he can, but you'd be able to get to her first, and time might be important."

Mr. Irwin saddled Courage for Tami and helped her astride. "Follow the trail," he advised, "and yell out her name real loud. Good luck to you."

Tami's heart was pounding wildly as she tried to remember all the horseback riding tips she had ever heard. *Keep your back straight. Keep your weight slightly forward. If you want to turn left, shift your weight to the left. To go right, press your right knee. . . .* All the advice was a jumble in her brain.

As Courage headed for the trail, Tami leaned forward and whispered desperately, "Please, Courage, find her! *Please!*"

At first, Courage moved slowly down the trail, but then he broke into a trot. Swallowing her panic, Tami hung on, shouting Aneal's name.

"Aneal! Aneal!" she yelled.

But the horse was going too fast! How could she get him to slow down? Now Courage was actually *galloping* down the dusty trail, his hooves kicking up clods of dirt. Tami was afraid that she would fly off at any moment. She imagined cracking her head on one of the boulders that lined the trial.

"Slow down!" Tami shouted. "Oh, Courage, *please* slow down!" But the big gray and white horse galloped on.

Tami racked her brain in an effort to remember the riding instructions. *Shift your weight slightly backward. Squeeze with your legs. Use the reins to slightly increase pressure on the horse's mouth.*

Tami's face broke out in a cold sweat as the rocky landscape flew past.

Chapter 9

Tami could hardly believe it when Courage slowed to a trot!

"It worked, it worked!" she told herself gratefully. She was shaking so hard that the reins almost fell from her grasp. Then she recovered her voice and started shouting Aneal's name once again.

"Aneal! Where are you?" Tami yelled with all her might.

"Over here," a child's voice called out. Aneal was sitting atop a large, smooth boulder. "I got tired," she said, "so I stopped to take a little rest."

As Aneal started to climb down from the giant rock, Tami heard a strange, buzzing sound from the brush at the foot of the boulder. She knew that rattlesnakes lived here in the lower elevations. Could that actually be a rattlesnake in the tall weeds just below Aneal's dangling feet?

"Don't move!" Tami shouted, "don't move an inch! I'm coming, Aneal."

But first Tami had to get off the big horse. She didn't know how. Tami held the reins and gingerly swung her leg over the horse. Then she clumsily dropped to the ground, nearly falling on her face. The startled horse almost reared up, but Tami hung onto the reins and led him to a small tree, tying the reins firmly.

Then Tami began walking slowly toward the boulder where Aneal sat waiting. *"Don't move,"* Tami said again. She could see it now—a huge rattlesnake with its telltale diamond pattern and large rattle. The grass was moving as the snake crawled from under the boulder. Its enormous body seemed to lumber along like a miniature freight train with many cars. "Don't move, Aneal!" Tami repeated in a deliberately calm voice.

"Why not?" Aneal asked.

"There's a rattlesnake at the bottom of the boulder. I don't want you to upset him," Tami explained.

"A *real* rattlesnake?" Aneal said with more curiosity than fear. "Wow! Show me! Where is it?"

"Aneal, *don't move!* Snakes strike at moving objects," Tami said. She had learned that bit of snake lore during counselor orientation.

When the rattlesnake had finally gone off into the grass, Tami hurried to Aneal. Taking her hand, she helped the little girl down from the boulder. "I want you to come back to camp now."

"Back to camp? But what about going to Cottonwood?" Aneal asked.

"Your father can find you at camp," Tami said. "We're having a wonderful shish-kebab barbecue tonight. I want you to sit at my table, okay?"

"I guess so," Aneal said.

With a mighty heave, Tami boosted Aneal up on Courage's back. Then she climbed on herself, feeling almost as nervous as before.

"How come you're shaking, Tami?" Aneal asked.

"I told you I was scared of horses," Tami said.

"Don't be scared," Aneal said. "I'll help you tell Courage what to do."

"Thanks, Aneal," Tami said.

"Tami, if you're so scared of horses, how come you got on Courage and followed me?" Aneal asked.

"Because I was *worried* about you, Aneal," Tami said sternly. "I was afraid you'd slip and fall into a canyon, or that a snake would bite you. You shouldn't have come out here by yourself. *Somebody* had to come get you —and there was nobody else but me. I'm not brave, but I had to do it."

"Well, *I* think you're brave, Tami. Grandma told me that when you do something you're really scared of, then you're brave. One time I was scared to go to the dentist. But I went anyway, and Grandma said that proved I was brave. Grandma says that only scared people who go ahead in spite of their fear can be called brave," Aneal said.

Tami smiled. She reached down and patted Courage's silky mane. "Courage is brave, too, isn't he? After all, his leg hurt, and he must have known that he was being ridden by a foolish girl. But he came through, didn't he?"

By the time Tami and Aneal rode into camp, the sheriff had arrived, and a search party was being organized. A big cheer went up when everyone saw Aneal riding with Tami.

At the shish-kebab barbecue that evening, Tami's rescue of Aneal was the main topic of conversation. Dane Morgan sat beside Tami. "You sure overcame your fear of horses today, Tami. When push came to shove, you came through with flying colors."

Tami smiled. "I guess I was more worried about Aneal than I was about riding. But I *still* don't feel comfortable on top of a horse," she laughed.

As Tami walked to her tepee that night, it dawned on her that she didn't have a girlfriend to talk to about her day. At the barbecue, she had glanced around at the faces of the other counselors, but everybody seemed to have made friends already. Tami would have felt funny pushing her way into one of the cozy little circles that were already formed.

"But," Tami told herself, "I have to start somewhere. When I get to college, everybody I meet will be a stranger. I *must* learn how to reach out. I don't want to huddle down in Little Vietnam for my entire life. . . ."

Chapter 10

Outside her tepee, Tami noticed a girl with long blonde hair. She looked nice enough. Tami wondered if she had enough nerve to start a conversation. It made her nervous just to think about it, but she forced herself. "Hi," Tami called. "I'm Tami. You're the girl who teaches the origami class, aren't you? The children in my cabin really like that class. . . ."

The girl stared at Tami, smiled, and then saw another counselor coming up the path. In another second the blonde girl and her friend were happily chatting with each other as they walked back down the path.

Tami felt embarrassed. She was sorry she had opened her mouth. It seemed to happen like that so often. Whenever she tried to talk to people, it all went wrong. Somehow they didn't seem interested in knowing her.

Before Tami turned and went into the tepee, a figure came from a row of tepees nearer the lake. It was Sommer. She had had a bad day. On the horseback ride, Dane had ignored her. Then, at the barbecue, she'd seen him sitting with Tami. She was burning with resentment.

"There you are, Tami. I suppose you think you're a big shot because you went after that kid," Sommer said bitterly. "But the truth is that nobody is all that impressed. Vanessa and I only let you hang out with us at school because you were so pathetic. But you have to face it—people don't like you, and they never will!"

Fighting tears, Tami hurried into the tepee and closed the door. She knew that she should ignore Sommer. She pretended she hadn't even heard her cruel words. But each one had struck Tami like a blow. Maybe what Sommer said was true. Maybe she would *never* find her own nice friends. Maybe she would always be lonely, on the outside looking in.

At breakfast the next morning, Tami stared down at her scrambled eggs. She was determined not to embarrass herself again by approaching another stranger. But when she looked up she saw a friendly looking girl with short, curly black hair and big eyes. The girl was talking to another girl, but she looked very happy and bubbly—like the sort of person with a big enough heart to make room for *many* friends, not just one or two.

Tami thought about it. Should she take one more chance? Should she risk another snub, another hurt? Could she find the courage to try one more time? She remembered what Aneal had said about bravery. She remembered what Grandfather had told her. And she thought about the courage it had taken to ride the big gray and white horse even though she was shaking with fear. . . .

"Hi," she finally said. "I'm Tami."

"Hi," smiled the girl. "I'm Alicia. Where's your tepee?"

"I'm in Tepee F," Tami said.

"Then we're almost neighbors! I'm right around the bend in Tepee H. Hey, what are you and your kids doing later on? I'm an astronomy nut. I want to take the kids out to study the stars tonight. You want to bring your girls, too, Tami? I think we'll have fun. I baked some moon cookies. They're just big round white sugar cookies, but calling them moon cookies is more fun," Alicia said with a giggle.

"That sounds really good," Tami said excitedly. "I work in the kitchen, so I can bring lemonade for us to drink and some paper cups."

"Oh, wow, would you?" Alicia said.

"Sure," Tami said.

Alicia grinned. "This is *great*! I've been here for three days now, and I haven't made any real good friends. How come you and I didn't find each other sooner?" She threw her arm around Tami's shoulders.

"I—I don't know," Tami said. She was so surprised and overcome with joy that she could barely speak.

"I'll get the moon cookies and meet you outside about nine then, Tami. You bring your girls and the lemonade. I can hardly wait. This is gonna be fun!" Alicia said.

A few hours later, when the star-watching party was underway, Alicia said, "Let's get together tomorrow and make planetariums with our kids? Oh, but you probably want to go horseback riding. I heard about what you did today. And I know there's another ride scheduled for tomorrow."

"Oh, no, I'm scared of horses," Tami said quickly. "I'd *love* to work on a planetarium!"

"*You, too?*" Alicia giggled. "You mean it's not just me? I've been afraid to tell a living soul how terrified I am of horses!"

The two girls threw their arms around each other, laughing.

Sitting nearby, Aneal couldn't help overhearing the conversation between the two counselors. And she couldn't help laughing along with them—even with her mouth full of moon cookies.

COMPREHENSION QUESTIONS

RECALL

1. Why did Tami Nguyen take the job as a camp counselor?

2. What happened to make Vanessa and Sommer turn away from Tami?

3. What secret fear was embarrassing to Tami?

ANALYZING CHARACTERS

1. Why did Tami ask to be assigned as a kitchen helper?

2. What two words could describe Sommer? Explain your thinking.
   - *spiteful*
   - *compassionate*
   - *vain*

3. What two words could describe Aneal? Explain your thinking.
   - *lonely*
   - *superstitious*
   - *insecure*

VOCABULARY

1. What kind of horse would be called *spirited*?

2. Sommer and Vanessa tried to *humiliate* Tami in front of Dane Morgan. What does *humiliate* mean?

3. Aneal's parents were involved in a fight over *custody* of their daughter. What is *custody*?

DRAWING CONCLUSIONS

1. When Sommer said that Dane had complained about Tami's whining, what conclusion did Tami draw?

2. What conclusion did Tami draw about how she got trapped in the barn?

3. What conclusion had Tami reached about approaching strangers?